Six Short Stories on the
VIA DOLOROSA

By
Ernesto V. Laguette

Published by
THE RIEHLE FOUNDATION
P.O. Box 7
Milford, Ohio 45150

Published by The Riehle Foundation

For additional copies of this book, individuals should contact the publisher:

The Riehle Foundation
P.O. Box 7
Milford, Ohio 45150
1-513-576-0032

Bookstores and book distributors contact:
Faith Publishing Company
P.O. Box 237
Milford, Ohio 45150
1-800-576-6477

Library of Congress Catalog Card No.: 94-061407

ISBN: 1-877678-29-5

Scripture quotations from *The New American Bible.*

Illustrations from "Portrait of the Passion" and "A Touch of Grace," by Catholic Treasures, 626 Montana Street, Monrovia, CA 91016. We gratefully acknowledge their permission to use illustrations.

Table of Contents

	Typed Pages	Illustration Pages
Dedication	iv	
Acknowledgements	v	vi
Foreword	vii	

* * *

The Scourger	1	2
Simon	13	14, 17, 20, 22
Veronica	25	29, 38
Gamaliel	43	44, 46
Longinus	55	56, 58
Dismas	67	
The Stations of the Cross	77	

Dedication

To my beloved wife, Doris,

who gave me the best years

of her life and opened my

heart to Jesus;

and to my children

Ernest, Lisa and Paul

who helped me overcome my

grief through her death.

To Stephen and Anne,

who helped me carry my cross.

Acknowledgements

These short stories would be incomplete without grateful acknowledgement of support and assistance from my family, friends and associates from the prayer groups that I attend. Thank you for your encouragement.

Without Kay Sentovich, I could not have written any stories, her excellent proofreading and editing made it possible.

To all of you who had the patience to read my stories and took the time to encourage me to continue writing.

Foreword

Whenever I read in the New Testament of Our Lord's Passion, or when I pray and meditate the sorrowful mysteries of the Rosary, I think about the people that were present, and wonder what their thoughts, feelings, and emotions were. They were blessed people, and they were sinners like us. They felt pain and joy, sorrow and happiness. They had to face life after seeing Jesus' sufferings. Also, I ask many questions which can never be answered; like what happened to them? Did they all convert, and did Our Lord Jesus forgive them, etc. . . ?

It took me several months to read all five volumes of *The Poem of the Man-God* by Maria Valtorta. Hundreds of characters are identified in this masterpiece of literature. Some of the characters are described in detail throughout, while some are vaguely mentioned. It contains vivid details of their actions, but little about the course of their lives.

I always wanted to write biblical short stories. So, I decided to write about Simon the Cyrene. There is hardly anything written about this man that helped Jesus carry His cross. I tried to write, to reflect on what occurred to him. I made a pest of myself with my family and all my friends. After I finished it, I gave them copies and requested their comments. No one gave me negative comments. In fact, some encouraged me to write other stories and recommended having them published. So, I decided to write.

The stories which I have written are only on six persons mentioned in Our Lord's Passion: a portrait of their possible personal feelings, conversion, acceptance or rejection of Jesus, the conflicts they faced, and how they resolved them. They all were in God's plan of Salvation, most of all in the Mercy of Jesus throughout their lives. I cannot single out anyone special. We **all** are special in God's plan. Our lives are a daily number of decisions to accept God's will. He never interferes in our road to holiness and salvation. We have to trust in His mercy.

Veronica is probably the one most admired woman of the Holy Women that followed Jesus, second to Mary Magdalene. I perused through the five volumes of *The Poem of the Man-God* and selected episodes and summarized some of them in my third short story. I tried to take her place and feel what she felt, and to express her emotions. A book could have been written based only on her story. There are several short stories, legends, and fables about her already written.

My first story is titled "The Scourger." It is about one of the soldiers that scourged Our Lord. Nothing is known about him. His name is unknown. If known, no one would want to be named after him. Was he also one of the Roman soldiers that crucified Our Lord? I could not write about the crucifixion. I experienced deep sorrow in describing the scourging. I do not know, sometimes, how I was able to do it. I prayed in order to write.

My fifth story titled "Longinus," is also about another soldier. There were many other Roman soldiers involved in Our Lord's Passion. The tomb guards, they must have had questions about Jesus?

My last story titled "Dismas," is about the thief that stole Heaven. There are many legends about him, but little is known about his life. Dismas consoled Our Lord on the cross and repented for his crimes. Our Lord in His Mercy forgave him. We all are Dismas. We all are unworthy. We must accept our suffering, repent, and ask for forgiveness.

There are so many short stories that can be written about other people, I list some below:

The Eleven Apostles	Eleven stories of despair, except for John; his is of courage.
Mary Magdalene	Many historical facts are documented and there are many books about her.
The Holy Women	Very special and unique—love.
The other thief	Rejection and evil.
Pilate	Did he commit suicide? What happened to him?
Claudia	Pilate's wife. Did she convert?
Caiaphas	Worse than Pilate, he knew what he did.
Nicodemus	Was he a martyr?

There are many more!

I found great joy and peace in writing these six short stories. It brought me closer to Jesus and to Our Blessed Virgin Mary.

I was somehow troubled writing about "Gamaliel," a learned man who could not recognize Jesus. Only by prayer was I able to overcome the obstacles.

These stories, of course, have to be treated as fictional accounts. How could they be otherwise? We have no knowledge, no history of what happened to these people. Then again. . .

You might identify yourself in some parts of these six stories. It is our human nature. And if we accept that what we are is by the grace of God, then we should be thankful for our faith, hope, and charity and that we weren't actually present.

May Our Lord Jesus grant you graces to continue on your daily conversion to holiness and eternal life! Praise be Jesus and Mary!

1

The Scourger

In a short time I will be dead. Not by my own hand but by the hands of my comrades, because I no longer want to behave like them and be what I was. I have been scourged and now I am tied to a wooden board, where I will be used as a target and be killed by lances. I have never been afraid of death. I had always thrived on killing, maiming and torturing with no remorse or conscience until the last few months. My life had been based on cruelty and hate. In these few moments that I await death, I feel a deep sorrow and remorse for all I have done in my life. I am only afraid of what I will face when I die—what my soul will face. The sorrow that I feel gives me hope and faith that I will be saved by the mercy of the God Almighty, and by His forgiveness. I did not know what I was doing. I did not know better until recently. This is my story.

I do not know where to start. I do not remember my mother or father. I know I never had paternal or

maternal love, or any kind of love, only hate. I remember being raised by strangers and all that I remember is that I would always run away from those who tried to take care of me. I took to the streets of Rome when I was a child and joined a gang of children who survived by crime. I learned to depend only on my wits and strength.

It is best that my name is not known. It is a Jewish name so I must be of Jewish descent. I speak Hebrew but I do not remember when or where I learned it.

As I grew older, I committed all kinds of crimes and was always in trouble. I became a gang leader and feared by those that knew me because of my cruelty. My gang was also feared and we had the run of the city until I made a mistake. I was caught killing a woman and imprisoned. A choice was given to me while in prison: join Tiberus' Army or be sent to a mine for the rest of my life. I was a strong and healthy young man.

I made the only choice and became a soldier. I needed very little training, but I had to learn how to obey orders and soon I was marching throughout the numerous countries conquered by the Roman Legions. I became a fearless soldier and my reputation of cruelty grew in bounds. Two years ago I was ordered to go to Jerusalem, in Judea, to be part of detachment of soldiers under Pontius Pilate because of my Jewish background. My duty was to interrogate prisoners—if necessary by torture. I became an expert at inflicting pain.

I did not believe in gods or life after death. I was a man without a soul. I lived only for the present which was debauchery, fornication, murder, drunkenness, selfishness, anger, and everything connected with evil. I became friends with a man in my detachment named Clement, who was just as cruel as I. His name should have been Inclement. We took turns to see who could inflict the most pain without killing the prisoners. We were feared by all the prisoners and by the rest of the soldiers in our detachment.

There were days when I would not even remember my name. I would be drunk for days at a time. I was like a possessed man with no honor or shame until that **Man** was brought to us to be scourged. I will never forget that fateful day. This **Man** had already been interrogated by Pilate. Clement and I were instructed not to keep count of the customary forty scourges (if we miscounted we would be scourged, two for one), but for us not to kill Him (if we killed the prisoner we would be scourged the full count of forty). We were ordered to make His appearance as pitiful as possible. He was to be brought back to Pilate for more questioning.

I had heard many things about this prisoner and I was curious and apprehensive at the same time. I had heard many rumors from the Jewish people about this **Man.** They called Him their "Savior." I did not understand their religion, so I did not try to understand what Savior meant.

As they brought the prisoner in the pillar court I took a good look at Him. He showed signs of already having been mistreated. He had a large bruise on His right cheek and a bloody nose. I was impressed by His calm and resigned attitude. He showed no fear. He had a distinct dignified appearance that I had never seen. I could not look at His eyes. If I looked at His eyes, I felt revulsion for myself. I had to turn away from Him; His demeanor filled me with rage and hate.

I said to myself—"He will be begging for mercy before we are through with Him." I was going to enjoy hurting Him. I was eager to start the scourging. I selected from the various whips, a Roman *flagrum*. This is a special whip with leather straps fitted with pairs of small balls made of lead. It inflicts the most painful and bloody scourges. It was forbidden to use it on Roman citizens, because of its savagery.

Instead of tying Him to a pillar, I hung Him by His wrists from a ring on an archway. We took off His clothes and He let us tie and hang Him without any protest. His toes barely touched the marble floor of the court. Hanging Him in this manner, Clement and I would be able to scourge Him at the same time, front and back, without untying Him.

I was the first to start the scourging by whipping His back. I could not face Him. Not a cry came out of His mouth, only the arching of His body as the whip cut His flesh and curled around His naked body. I wanted Him to cry but He did not. He endured the harsh punishment without a complaint. It made me furious. I had to stop. I was afraid to kill Him. I let Clement take over. He concentrated in slashing His arms and legs. I sensed he also had the same hate I had for the prisoner because his fury was merciless. Together we scourged Him and we lost count of the number of lashes.

We had to stop to clean the blood that had dripped from His body on the marble floor to avoid slipping. His body was completely covered with deep lacerations and we were ordered to stop after He fainted from the excruciating pain. At first, they thought that we had killed Him. I cannot recall ever scourging anyone so hard and unmercifully. It was unbelievable that He was alive. We were ordered to stop the scourging.

As He came to, we untied Him and dressed Him with a scarlet military cloak. I offered Him some water, which He drank eagerly. I never had been kind to any prisoner but I felt a respect toward Him—a respect for His courage and patience. I was able to look at His eyes and they were covered with tears. Clement swore and threw a bucket full of water at me, which also splashed the prisoner.

The Roman centurion who brought the prisoner to us, and who was waiting for the scourging to be finished, started to mock Him and decided to inflict more pain by weaving a crown of thorns from a thorn bush, crowning Him and calling Him "King of the Jews." The pain from the crown must have been insufferable. Drops of blood flowed in His already wounded face. The rest of the soldiers in the court followed the charade, spat on Him, slapping His face and calling Him the most obscene names. I was too tired to do anything and sat at the end of the court and watched.

I had vent all my anger and hate already on the prisoner, and yet, I had given Him some water. They were worse than animals. They forced Him to hold a reed in His right hand and made Him walk. Finally the

Roman centurion took Him away. As I saw Him walk away I felt pity and admiration for Him. I did not pay attention if His name had been said. I preferred not to learn or know anything about the prisoners or their names.

I kept trying to remember His name which I knew but I had forgotten. Also, to learn what had happened to Him. There was something very special about this Man. That afternoon, after the scourging, an eclipse and an earthquake occurred. I learned His name, Jesus Christ, and that on the same afternoon, He had been condemned to be crucified and was forced to carry His cross and died. He had claimed to be the Son of God. Also, I learned that the soldiers who guarded His tomb claimed that He had resurrected three days after. I spoke to the guards and verified that they had indeed seen Him walk away, resurrected. I did not believe them. It was the first time I started to have questions about life, religion, God, good and evil and the desire to know more about Jesus.

That night after I had learned about Jesus' resurrection, I had a nightmare or a vision; all I can recall is that I was surrounded by fire and by damned souls yelling and suffering. It happened for three consecutive nights. The fourth night it was a different dream or vision. I dreamed of Jesus Christ bathed in light with His arms stretched out, beckoning me. I was confused and disturbed. I did not want to go back to sleep or to understand what I was dreaming, so I took the easy way out. I got drunk with Clement.

I asked Clement if he had had any unusual dreams.

He replied, "Yes!" He was having terrible dreams and nightmares like I was about the Man we scourged. We are not the most intelligent or educated. All we wanted was to forget what we both had felt for the first time in our lives, a conscience. I had never prayed to any god, or cared to. There were so many gods and idols. Clement could not give me any answers, nor could I help him. I told him all I knew about Jesus Christ. He did not want to hear any of it.

The next few weeks changed my life. It was like God was giving me a chance to turn my life around. I saw what I was and it was a repugnant feeling. I had to make the choice. Good or Evil. The dreams stopped when I decided to pray. Pray! How? I tried and it filled me with remorse but at the same time with peace. I prayed to Jesus, not knowing why, and asked for His forgiveness.

I could no longer interrogate or torture prisoners; in them I saw Jesus. Clement sensed what was happening to me and ridiculed me and reported me. I was like a caged lion, undecided and perplexed. Jesus must have heard my prayers. Longinus, the commanding officer heard about my conflict and assigned me to the stables. I was demoted but I did not care. I found peace in shoveling the dung and cleaning the stables.

Taking risks at night, I searched and approached some of Jesus' disciples. I wanted to talk to the resurrected Jesus. To my amazement, they told me that Jesus had ascended into Heaven forty days after His resurrection. I was heart broken, but they explained to me about Jesus, Heaven and Hell, and eternal life. They gave me

answers to many of my questions. I had several meet-
ings with them and I began to firmly believe in God,
in Jesus Christ and His message. I never told them who
I was. I felt good for the first time in my life. The disciples were very understanding and gave me love, which
I accepted wholeheartedly. Also, for the first time in
my life I was expressing love by hugging them when
I departed. I wanted to go out in the streets and pro-
claim the name of Jesus, which I could not do.

It was happening so fast! They told me to contact
Peter, Jesus' chief apostle. They arranged a meeting place
where I could talk to Peter in private. I was told to
be cautious and to tell no one about the meeting. The
disciples were being persecuted. I awaited anxiously
for the meeting.

It was late at night and I took precautions not to
be followed. Peter was alone and waiting for me. He
looked like a warrior, husky and tall, but kind. He had
the same dignity I saw in Jesus. I trusted him immediately and approached him with confidence. He greeted
me with a smile and a hug:

"Peace be with you, brother. Tell me about yourself.
I have heard wonderful things about you."

With tears in my eyes I told him, who I was: "I am
a Roman soldier, one of Jesus' scourgers." He did not
show repulsion; instead he calmly held my hands. I
emptied my heart to him and told him all that had
happened to me—the visions and how I had decided
to change my life. But, I could not forgive myself for
what I had done to Jesus. He replied: "I did something
worse, I denied Him three times the night that He was

arrested, and I abandoned Him completely. He forgave me! Jesus came to save sinners, not to condemn us. He is love and mercy! He will forgive you, if you just ask Him."

"I have been praying to Him constantly and I have asked for His forgiveness many times. I feel unworthy and confused. I want to be saved."

"By obedience to the truth you have purified yourself by a genuine love for your brothers, therefore, love constantly from the heart. Your rebirth has come, not from a destructible but from an indestructible seed, through the living and enduring word of Jesus. You are a jewel and precious in His eyes. There is a cause for rejoicing here. You may for a time have to suffer the distress of many trials; but this is so that your faith, which is more precious than the passing splendor of fire-tried gold, may by its genuineness lead to praise, glory, and honor because you are achieving faith's goal, your salvation. Become holy yourself in every aspect of your conduct, after the likeness of Jesus who called you. Realize that you were delivered from the futile ways of your life by Christ's blood beyond all price (1 Peter 1:22, 23, 6, 7, 9). Do you believe in Him?"

"Yes, I do! With my whole heart!"

"Kneel down!"

I did and he laid his hands on my head. I closed my eyes and felt an overflowing warmth on my entire body.

"I baptize you Azarius in the name of the Father, Jesus Christ and the Holy Spirit. All your sins have been forgiven. Go in peace and sin no more! Do honor to your new name, it means 'God helps.' Ask for the Holy Spirit to guide you. Do not stifle the Holy Spirit and do not despair. Trust in the Lord!"

I finally felt the forgiveness and peace I had been seeking since I had decided to change my life. I began to believe in myself and to forget the past. I went back to my quarters with hope and relief. I liked my new name! I was reborn! Now I understand the dream that I had and why Jesus beckoned me. He gave me the grace and help to repent and in His gentleness, to freely make a choice to follow Him. He gave the same option to Clement, who chose not to. I showed pity and gave Him a few drops of water and He flooded me with **Love** and it allowed my heart to be opened. I was sick and He healed me. With a contrite heart I gave Him thanks and praise. I dare not rely on my own worth, but only on His mercy. I did what He asked me to do and I am prepared to die with great trust in His goodness.

A few days after, as I was cleaning the stables, I heard a commotion and yelling from one of the prison cells. I went to investigate and saw soldiers taking turns raping a young girl prisoner and her mother. I tried to stop them. Clement was one of them and he lunged at me with a knife. In the fight that ensued, Clement fell on the knife and I was pulled away. He died shortly after. I was court-martialed and sentenced to die. The irony of it all! I could not be crucified because I was a Roman soldier. Instead I was to be scourged and tied to a wooden board and killed by those that raped the women.

I waited patiently for the scourging. As my last request I asked that they use the same whips that were used on Jesus, which they allowed. Only twenty-five lashes were counted. During the scourging I kept praying to Jesus for His mercy and forgiveness. I accepted the scourging in atonement for my sins and I forgave my scourger and comrades. Jesus have mercy on them!

As the soldiers assembled to throw the lances, I gave thanks to Jesus for granting me the grace to follow Him, for letting me repent for my sins, which were worse than the scourging I inflicted on Him. The blood and tears He shed were not only for me, but for the sins of the whole world. Thank You, Jesus! I love You! Have mercy on me!

2

Simon

My name is Simon. It is Passover week, and my sons and I arrived two days ago in Jerusalem. It is Friday morning. This is the third time we made the pilgrimages from Cyrene.

It was a very long journey. We have been to various stores to purchase items we need for the Passover Supper. We finally located the last item—candles. I have never seen Jerusalem so crowded. It is almost noon time, and the heat is suffocating and the noise from the crowd coming toward us is frightening. I do not understand why the crowd is behaving so wildly. I heard that three criminals are to be crucified this afternoon. I do not want to see any of it. It is the worst punishment that can be inflicted on any man. I do not want my two sons, Alexander and Rufus, to witness any part of it. The Romans use this punishment only on rebels and the worst criminals.

We are in the middle of a noisy procession led by Roman soldiers. It is the crucifixion of the three and

And bearing the cross for
Himself, He went forth.
            John 19:17

we cannot get away! We are blocked by the oncoming yelling crowd. We have a donkey that is loaded with gifts and articles for the Passover Supper. We cannot move. The streets are too narrow and crowded and my two sons and I cannot escape.

I have never feared anything in my life, but now, for the first time, I feel fear. It is not only the crowd, the Roman soldiers and the three prisoners, but I sense an evil, dark, showering cloud falling and drowning everyone in the procession. It is like hades flooding Jerusalem. The insults and obscene gestures from the rioting crowd are the worst I have ever witnessed or heard. I want to run away but I cannot. I cannot leave my two sons and the loaded donkey.

"You with the donkey," yells a Roman soldier, "Come over here and help the prisoner carry His cross." I ignore his command, but he approaches me defiantly with his bare sword and motions for me to obey his command. I do not hesitate any longer. Angrily I order my sons, "Take the donkey and go to an empty street and wait for me, I will find you later on, one way or the other."

The crowd lets me in and I look at the prostrate prisoner whom I had avoided looking at before, and instead of repulsion or hate toward Him, because I am being forced to help Him, I feel pity and sorrow for Him. I do not want to run away anymore, I want to help Him. He has been scourged and is wearing a bloody crown of thorns. His left eye is almost closed from an injured and inflamed cheek. His nose is broken and bleeding. His body is all bruised, sweaty and bloody.

Every single place in His body must hurt. How can a man endure so much suffering! I try to help Him up but He stops me with a kind glance and with a soft smile, hardly distinguishable because of His bruises, a kindness which I have never felt from any man before. His eyes tell it all. He wants to get up by Himself. He takes the cross and I reluctantly take the foot of the cross and lift it to help him.

I am a strong man and I cannot believe this battered man is carrying the heavier part of the cross. The Roman soldier must have selected me from the crowd because of my strength and stature. I have to stumble because of the cobblestones in the street and the ropes coming from the crosses of the other two prisoners. Instead of helping him I am handicapping Him. I have to learn how to carry the foot of the cross without tripping.

This prisoner cannot be a convict, a murderer or a rebel. The glance He gave me is not from a man that is brutal or evil like the other two.

I begin to pay attention to the yells of the crowd and the insults addressed to Him. Who is He? Do I know Him? His bloody and torn face is not recognizable. They are mocking Him and calling Him the Messiah! Now I know who He is. He is Jesus the Teacher! No! It cannot be! I had heard Him teach last year in the Temple and I know some of His disciples. How can it be? I rejected His teachings because they demand too much. "Love your enemies and forgive them!" Yet, I see Him now and not one word of hate is coming from His lips. The prophesies from the laws of Moses,

the prophets, and the psalms are beginning to make sense to me. Yes, He must be the Messiah! Our Savior! How blind I have been by not listening to Him! Love is the redeeming act! His kind glance and soft smile opened my heart. I took pity on Him. I was no longer resentful. He flooded me with love without saying a single word. Yes, He is the Son of God! I have to hold my temper against those yelling insults now that I know whom I am helping. I am beginning to understand some of the prophesies—it is written that the Messiah must suffer. Yes, love is suffering! If you cannot love, you cannot suffer. Now I begin to feel all my unworthiness and all my sins by being near Him. I wish I had an army of warriors to defend Him. To save Him from the cross! No! Where are all His followers and disciples? Is He completely abandoned? My questions are answered immediately.

He falls again and a group of women surround Him. The Roman soldiers take pity on them and allow them to go near Him. He talks to them and He is consoling them instead of them consoling Him. One of them wipes His bruised and sweaty face with a soft cloth and leaves sobbing. The mob ridicules the sobbing woman and forces the soldiers to continue with the cruel procession. He gets up again by Himself; I do not dare to touch Him. I am not worthy.

We are headed toward a small mount on the dusty outskirts of Jerusalem called Golgotha. It can be seen not far away. It is getting hotter and hotter, Jesus is growing weaker and feverish. We hardly take a few steps and He falls again. A single woman and a young man about the same age as my older son come near him. She is His mother. The Roman on duty allows her and the young man to remain with Him and orders me to take the cross away from Him and to carry it by myself. I do not have to! He stands and moves a step away from the cross. Now I obey without hesitation! To my bewilderment, I find the cross very heavy. I hesitate for a minute until I realize that I do not want to move. I want to stop this procession. A soldier notices my hesitation and immediately whips me ferociously. Jesus looks at me again without saying a word and nods for me to move. I find the strength to carry it and I continue to the top of Golgotha.

The last steps are the hardest. I have to avoid rocks and holes and the climb is steep. I do not want to let go of the cross as we arrive. The crowd is wild now; the Roman soldiers have to call for reinforcements to control it and as soon as they arrive, they clear the area where the crucifixion is going to take place. I am forced by the Roman soldier in charge to let go of the cross and leave. But, before I leave, the young man that accompanies Jesus' mother gives me a soft tap on the shoulder, as to give me thanks. I look at Jesus for the last time, who is standing alone, still with the rope from the cross tied to His waist. His eyes meet my eyes and I start sobbing.

I never sobbed or cried before! What is happening to me? I always took pain and sorrow without a tear. I did not cry when my mother died, but now the pain of seeing Jesus all beaten, bloody, sweaty, and suffering and to be crucified overwhelms me with sorrow. I softly

murmur, "Jesus, I love You." There is nothing more that I can do! I turn my back to Him. I cannot look at Him any longer and slowly descend from the mount of Golgotha. As I do, I can hear the hammering of the nails on the cross. I cannot look back or wait for what is to happen next. I cannot stop sobbing.

I have to look for my two sons. It is going to take a miracle to find them. As I make my way through the mob I hear the voice of my older son Alexander calling me, "Father. . .Father. . ." I see them both and thank God both are okay. They approach me fearfully because they disobeyed my last order. I do not say one word. Sobbing I hug them both. They too start sobbing. They saw what I had done and sense something has happened to me. They feel the same sorrow that I have and try to console me. Without a word we slowly walk—holding each other—to the house of my relatives where we are staying.

It is months since the crucifixion. We have returned to Cyrene after a short stay in Jerusalem. All my family and I are Christian and many of my friends, whom I helped to convert. I am a different man from what I used to be before Golgotha. I have learned how to love and how to forgive, but more important, to avoid sin and live a Christian life. My children no longer fear me and we are a happy and loving family. Now I have sincere and loving friends.

The first thing I did upon returning to Cyrene was to visit the tomb of my father whom I hated very much. I did not attend his funeral, that much hate I had for

him. I knelt and asked for his forgiveness. I know he
has forgiven me.

Life is much different now that I believe in Jesus
Christ and His teaching. He did not say one word to
me during those few agonizing minutes on the walk
to Golgotha. He did not have to! He taught me by His
silence that each one of us must live and face Golgotha by ourselves, where He carried each of our crosses
that we are reluctant to carry. We must stumble and
trip as we learn to carry only the foot of the cross with
Him, and once we learn how, then we must carry the
entire cross. He gives us the strength to carry it, no
matter how heavy it is. He never gives us a cross we
cannot carry. Now I do not complain or ask why; instead
I accept it and trust in the Lord, trust in His mercy
and love.

Many wonderful things have happened in my new
life since Golgotha, and I give thanks to Jesus every
day. Now I await anxiously the last final minute, when
I will see Him again, in all His glory, with His arms
outstretched welcoming me, and I will hear Him calling my name—Simon (obedient).

3

Veronica

The first time I met Jesus was the first time my heart was filled with a radiant love and an indescribable peace. I will never forget it as long as I live. It was not actually seeing Him, but what I felt in His presence. I sensed Him long before I saw Him. As He approached me, it was like my soul knew that He was the Creator, aching for His infinite love and surrendering to joy, happiness, great peace, and a sense of well-being, where there is no darkness but only light. I felt transported to another dimension. I was no longer part of this earth. Time no longer existed. I had to turn around to comprehend and search for what was approaching me. I could not understand it.

I was alone in the Temple praying. He entered into the hall surrounded by people. I saw Him and all my expectations were fulfilled. I understood then all the feelings and sensations I had. When His eyes met my eyes, no longer did I have to search for answers; it was Jesus, the Messiah. All my doubts were dispelled

in mind and soul. I was in the presence of the Son
of God!

I started to search for the Messiah last year, after
my husband died. My name is Veronica. I am a Roman
Jewess—a widow with means, thanks to my deceased
husband. I have no children, but my life has been full
of blessings. I have always tried to keep the commandments. My life has been more than comfortable. My
parents always provided for me and I was their only
child. My life has always been full of love. Then, my
husband, a very religious man and respected in the com-
munity, gave me all my needs and surrounded me with
servants. I have always been thankful for all that I have,
so I have dedicated my life to help the poor and destitute. Before dying, my husband made these last requests
from me: To pray for his soul to enter paradise, and
for me to return to Judea to search for the Messiah
and to do all I could do for Him. He prophesied that
all the nations will know my name. I did not face any
loneliness or feel abandoned being a widow. On the
contrary, I had a new purpose for my life and I pursued
it avidly. My husband somehow knew I would meet
the Messiah.

I tried to memorize the most important prophesies
proclaiming the coming of the Messiah. Isaiah gave
me enough clues of what I was to look for and what
to expect:

> *"There was in Him no stately bearings to
> make us look at Him, nor appearance that
> would attract us to Him. He was spurned and*

avoided by men, a man of suffering, ac-
customed to infirmity, one of those from
whom men hide their faces, spurned, and we
held Him no esteem. Yet it was our infirmi-
ties that He bore, our sufferings that He en-
dured, while we thought of Him as stricken,
as one smitten by God and afflicted...
Though He was harshly treated, He submit-
ted and opened not His mouth; Like a lamb
led to the slaughter or a sheep before the
shearers, He was silent and opened not His
mouth. Oppressed and condemned, He was
taken away..." (Isaiah 53:2b-4, 7-8a).

I had set up a home for the poor, orphans, widows and pilgrims in Jerico. I selected Jerico because of its proximity to Jerusalem, the Holy City, after hearing wonderful stories about a new prophet, Jesus, and how the Pharisees were constantly attacking Him. I met some of His disciples and they told me all about His teachings of eternal life, love and forgiveness, about healings and multiplication of bread and fish, and so many other miraculous events. I contacted other Jewesses of the Diaspora. They did not have any doubts that Jesus was the Messiah as foretold by the prophets. I believed them, so I stopped searching. All I had to do was to wait!

The events that followed were providential and not coincidental. As soon as I received news that Jesus was to arrive in Jerusalem, I rushed to the Temple and waited impatiently for His arrival. I knelt and kissed His feet. My joy in finally being near Him could not be contained.

I am not an emotional person but I wanted to touch Him, hug Him and never be separated from Him. I had to restrain myself. I did not feel worthy. He understood, and gently took my hand as I stood up. He knew who I was and asked from me what I wanted.

"To be your disciple and follow You, Jesus, my Lord," I replied and explained to Him why. He instructed me to go to Joanna, the wife of Chusa, Herod's steward.

I wanted to talk more to Him, but the people surrounding Him made it impossible. He proceeded to the main hall of the Temple to sacrifice His lamb. The Pharisees and Scribes promptly attacked His teachings and mocked Him. I could not stay to listen to their attack.

I immediately went to Joanna and she received me unquestionably after I told her of the instructions given by Jesus. She introduced me to the rest of the Holy Women who took care of the temporal needs of the Master and His apostles. She gave me the task of preparing new clothes, and asked me to return when I finished them. I was now part of the Holy Women. I did not question her direction. I returned to Jerico.

Four days later, in the early evening, the Master and His apostles dropped by unexpectedly at my large house in Jerico. What joy it was to see Our Lord again! My servants were surprised when I knelt and kissed His feet to welcome Him. This time I was not only able to talk to Jesus alone, but also to Peter. It was like I had known Peter all my life. His kindness is bigger than his rugged appearance. He is like a puppy, ready to give only love. His sincerity and honesty is over-

whelming. We talked about pride, and how afraid he
was of becoming proud. That, I believe, will never happen to him. Everyone enjoyed the food and rest. It was
an unforgettable evening. They retired early except for
the Master and myself.

My conversation with Our Lord was about what my
husband had requested of me and that I felt it was
a wrong decision to settle in Jerico, instead of follow-
ing Him. He gave me reassuring words about remaining in Jerico, and gave me a mission to fulfill. This
was to bring bread once a month to a penitent, or rather
"reviving man," in the hills of Cherith for a period of
less than twelve months. At the Feast of the Tabernacle onward, I was also to bring him four jars of oil and
at the Feast of the Tabernacle, a goat skin garment and
blanket; I was to be kind and greet him in the name
of Jesus of Nazareth in order to give him hope and
inspire him. It would be a sacrifice for me but merciful to the Master and to the penitent soul.

I realized when He said that it would be less than
twelve months, that the prophesies of Isaiah and David
would be fulfilled, and I started to weep. He kindly
took my hands to comfort me and I opened my heart
to Him and explained how I always read the prophets
with my husband, and how we shuddered with horror
at the words of David and Isaiah and asked Him if it
had to be like that for Him.

"Yes and worse..."

"No! No!...Who will console You? Where will You
find the fortitude?"

"From the love of My Mother and My disciples."

"Grant me the grace to be near You and the strength to console You. Permit me to share in Your suffering, so that my soul will also feel the pain. Let me look at Your face and let me wipe Your tears." I could not stop sobbing as I looked up at Him bathed in the bright light from the full moon.

"Veronica, you will be there and you shall give Me your compassion and more. Your name will be praised —In the hour of need she assisted her Lord."

The Master laid His hands on my head while I was getting up, and then we went into the silent house for our night's rest. His touch gave me the peace I needed.

The next few months were the happiest and most active of my life, and I completely forgot all about the sorrowful prophesies about Our Lord. Our Lord was right. My home in Jerico became a center of activity, a refuge of love for all those in need. I assigned a steward to take care of it when I had to be in Jerusalem to be with the Master, and to work with Joanna and with the Holy Women. Mary of Magdala taught me how to pray Our Lord's prayer, the "Our Father." We all had many tasks and duties and we were very busy instructing the proselytes and praying. Under the guidance of Joanna, we all worked in harmony and friendship. Eliza became my companion and we were inseparable.

There is something very special when women get together to talk and work for a purpose. Ours was to help the Master in all His needs and support His apostles. Our friendship knew no bounds. Our talks and discussions on the lessons from the Master were not controlled by a leader. We all had a common bond and understanding under the guidance of Our Lord. We were eager to exchange ideas freely without discord. Harmony and peace was our life. We were disciples learning the ways of Jesus.

Our happiest days were when we were with Our Lord and with Mary, His Mother. Mary was the example of what we women must be. We tried to imitate her humility, trust and compassion. We always went to her for counsel on personal problems. She never refused us and her counsel was always the best solution. We loved to pray with her and she was the one who always would ask us to pray.

Our Lord assigned me a young teenage girl and she became like a daughter to me. Our lives truly reflected Our Lord and His Mother—love. The more we gave, the more we received.

In Jerico, I was busy with my mission at the hill of Cherith and in aiding Zaccheus, the local tax collector. Zaccheus was a rich man who converted when Our Lord visited and stayed in his house. He had found it hard to be honest. He needed to trust in Our Lord. The temptations made him weak and lose confidence. He would visit me frequently and was able to regain his confidence through our long talks on the teachings of Our Lord. He realized that only by keeping the commandments would love remain in his heart, and then he could forgive those who made things hard for him.

It was his willingness that made him strong. Our

Lord visited him periodically and listened silently to what he had done. This, in turn, caused conversions in some of Zaccheus' friends. Jesus poured all His love on their emotional wounds. The reign of love is in our hands and it depends on how we treat and love all the people around us by imitating Our Savior.

My activities in Jerusalem increased after the Feast of the Tabernacle. The Pharisees' and Sadducees' attacks on Our Lord intensified, and rumors started to spread that He would be arrested. Sensing the danger Our Lord was facing every time He preached in the Temple, I decided to stay in a small house not far away from the southwest corner of the Temple.

Jesus performed one of the greatest miracles for the Pharisees, the Scribes and the Sadducees, a sign that they had demanded in Qedesh. This was the raising of the rotting dead body of Lazarus back to life. Still they did not believe in Him, but now, there were no more rumors about arresting Our Lord. A decree was issued for His arrest. He awaited His final hour away from Jerusalem, in Ephraim and Samaria, until Passover week. Our Lord, more than once, spoke to His apostles and disciples about His coming death, but no one wanted to believe or understand it.

He and His apostles made their last stop at my house in Jerico as they returned to Jerusalem for Passover Week. Over five hundred disciples waited for Him. It was an unforgettable and very sorrowful evening. Our Lord was seen with tears streaming from His eyes. When asked "why" by John, His youngest apostle, He explained that His thoughts were for Jerusalem, con-

templating a clucking hen that was protecting her
golden-hued chickens under her wings. He had covered
the nakedness of Jerusalem with His mantle just like
the hen with her wings, but Jerusalem had refused His
mantle, His love.

After a few days at Lazarus' house, Our Lord invited
all the women disciples and the Holy Women to come
to Bethany. Joanna sent a messenger for me to come
the Friday before Passover Week. We were, in all, fif-
teen women, and Our Lord started to talk to us and
said to us words of encouragement because in the next
few days we would face many hardships. He spoke to
us as a friend. The rest of His talk was full of love
and He admonished us not to weep in this last period
of His mortal life. He addressed and consoled each one
of us and encouraged us to face the future. We all wept
in silence.

All I could think of were the words in *Psalm* 22:17:

> *"Indeed, many dogs surround me, a pack
> of evildoers closes in upon me; They have
> pierced my hands and my feet; I can count
> all my bones..."*

We prayed to God Almighty for fortitude after He left
us. We remained in Lazarus' house until the start of Passover Week, and from there we watched His triumphant
entry into Jerusalem. "The Lamb of Salvation can be
slain only on the Passover of Unleavened Bread."

It had been twelve months and days from the first
time that I met Our Lord in the Temple. Paradise soon
would be opened!

There are different kinds of sorrow. There is also the divine sorrow which brings salvation and joy. It is mingled with repentance. It tempers the bitterness of the sorrow. It is full of hope. I was to share this divine sorrow and to be tormented with physical suffering and spiritual grief on Calvary, with the rest of the Holy Women.

Eve was the first to sin. Now it will be the role of the Holy Women to be the first to console and support Our Lord to atone for Eve's action. The role of women is about to be changed in regards to manners and treatment by society as well as with regards to many other things. And it will be unprejudiced, because Our Lord's Mother will obtain grace and redemption mainly for women, as Our Lord Jesus will do for all men. Women will also be the stronger of the disciples of Our Lord. They will be the ones that will pray unceasingly, perform more sacrifices, and willingly become victim souls.

It was on Friday morning that John the Apostle, who had followed what had happened to Our Lord after His arrest, and after pleading with God Almighty for courage, rushed to Mary, Our Lord's Mother, to tell her that Our Lord was on the way to Calvary to be crucified. Mary requested to be taken to Him as soon as possible and asked John to inform his mother and all the other women.

As soon as I received word from Joanna of what was happening, I rushed to Calvary with my young maidservant who carried for me a basket containing a change of clothes for Our Lord, which I had prepared, so that

He would not have to wear the rags of the executioners. I arrived in time to get close to Joanna and the rest of the Holy Women who surrounded Mary, Our Lord's Mother, and John, His youngest apostle. We all broke into tears upon seeing Our Lord, scourged, bleeding and carrying the cross. Weeping, we approached the cruel mob to get closer to Him. God Almighty, why does He have to suffer? Why? Why? I could not understand it! He gave us love, and we return inhuman and indescribable treatment.

He had been abandoned by all His followers and apostles, except for John. Were we the only ones to be near Him? The Roman Centurion waved at Mary and signaled her and all of us to approach Jesus, who had fallen carrying the cross, and momentarily allowed to rest. Temporarily, I was held back by the crowd and unable to get close to Jesus. In this brief moment, my only thought was "what can I do for Our Lord?"

Without hesitation, I told my maidservant to give me the loin cloth made of the finest linen. It would be cool enough to wipe His face. Without fear, I pushed the people around me and bravely forced myself to get as close as possible to Jesus. Many tried to stop me but I pushed back. I was not afraid and did not listen to their insults or ridicule. His eyes met my eyes and I started sobbing, but I offered Him the cloth.

He managed to hold it with one hand and I helped Him to wipe His face, avoiding the crown's thorns. He felt the relief of the cool cloth and held it against His face. He handed me back the cloth with a faint smile—a smile that will be impressed in my mind for eternity.

I sensed it as a sign of love and my heart lept with
joy, for comforting Him. Thank You, Jesus, for giving
me the strength to be near You!

Jesus turned to the Holy Women and said:
*"Daughters of Jerusalem, do not weep for me. Weep
for yourselves and for your children. The days are coming when they will say, 'Happy are the sterile, the
wombs that never bore and the breasts that never
nursed'"* (Luke 23:28, 29)
We knelt down in adoration and He comforted each
of us by our names, thanking each one of us, and then
signaled us to leave. The crowd started to curse us and
mistreat us; the Roman soldiers made a path for us
to move away from Jesus.

We left Jesus behind; we could not continue the rest
of the walk of Calvary. Our grief was too deep for us
to remain and watch the crucifixion and death of Our
Lord.

Paulina, Lydia, Valeria (the Roman women) and my
servant surrounded me, fearing that the crowd might
attack me and take away the linen cloth. I hid it within
the folds of my dress. We arrived safely at my small
house near the temple. Still sobbing, and without a
word, the Roman women departed.

Exhausted with grief, I went to my bedroom and knelt
down crying and praying to God Almighty. I gave Him
thanks for giving me the courage to console my Lord.
All I could do is pray and pray.

Suddenly, an earthquake startled me. Our Lord must
be dead. . . and in fear, I fainted. As I came to, I rushed

to where the linen cloth was folded and to my bewilderment, I smelled the most heavenly scent. It was like a mixture of incense and myrrh. It did not smell of perspiration or blood. And as I unfolded it, I saw the impressed image of the bloody and disfigured Face of Jesus with a faint smile.

I knelt down in veneration. "Oh! Thank You, Jesus!. . . Thank You, Jesus!" Kneeling I continued to adore it. "What a beautiful gift! I cannot keep it! It is too precious! It belongs to Jesus' Mother. I must bring it to her. It will give her consolation."

I did not know what time it was, but I rushed to wake up my maidservant and a strong man I hired to protect the house, to accompany us to John's house where Mary would be staying, or maybe John knew where she might be. I had to find her, for she must have the linen cloth.

I can still recall the scene, and word for word, I can replay it in my mind. . .

It is very late at night and walking in fear, only in the dark shadows, we move through the streets. As we arrive, I knock at the door of John's house. I have to knock several times until, finally I hear the voice of a woman who asks:

"Who is there?"

"It is me, Veronica. Open quick!"

As the door opens, I see the Holy Women and John with an apprehensive look, and a question in their eyes without asking: What does she want?

"I have to see Mary, Our Lord's Mother. . ." Weeping

I say, "It is a gift from Our Lord."

They all surround me, they want to see the gift. I try to talk and I cannot. Finally, gasping for words, I start to explain about... "The loin linen cloth...Calvary...Seeing Our Lord all sweaty and bloody...Rushing to Him...Giving Him the cloth...Helping Him wipe His face...His faint smile...Taking back the cloth...Holding the cloth as a precious jewel...The Roman ladies protecting me and the cloth...Going back to my home...The earthquake and me fainting...Waking up...The scent from the linen cloth...The image of Our Lord...Venerating it... Thinking of Mary..."

"Show it to us! Show it to us!"

"No, it is only for Mary, Our Lord's Mother."

"She is extremely tired. She has not talked to anyone. She has been all alone sobbing, with the door closed," John replies.

"Knock at her door. Tell her it is I, with a gift from her Son. She will understand."

John does and she opens the door.

"Come in, Veronica!"

John enters first and I follow. John helps her to a chair. I give John the folded linen cloth and he unfolds it. The impressed image of Our Lord, His living face, looks at His Mother and she beams with joy. The rest of the Holy Women enter and we all prostrate ourselves in front of the unfolded cloth. "Jesus!... Jesus!... Jesus, we love You!"

Mary starts quietly to sob and we do too, amazed at the sorrowful beauty of the image.

"Thank You, God Almighty! Thank You, Holy Son!

The sign I was waiting for," Mary exclaims. She looks at me and gives me thanks.

I cannot say one word. I stand up and take the cloth from John's hands, kiss it and give it to her. Quietly I leave the room without turning my back to Mary. I do not want to break the solemnity of the moment. I go out in the night, closing behind me the door of John's house.

As we walked back to my home, I was no longer afraid to walk in the dark shadows of the night. My heart was full of joy. All I could feel was that I did what Our Lord wanted me to do, and I did it without Him telling me. It was in my heart. I remember His words to me: *"She assisted her Lord."* The sign His Mother was waiting for, to relieve Her sorrow, was in her hands, and now I understood what was awaiting mankind and what would happen in three days.

Paradise had been opened and His Resurrection would now take place, otherwise it all would have been in vain. What a glorious day awaited us! I had no doubts. Redemption would soon be completed. Praised be God Almighty!

Episodes, condensed, were taken in part from Valtorta, Maria, *The Poem of The Man-God.* Centro Editoriole Valtortiano, Isola del Liri, Italy, 1989. English Translations.

4

Gamaliel

My soul has been aching to understand the many acts of futility in my life. With regret and sorrow, I remember many actions in my life which I should not have taken, but my vanity, pride and selfishness had blinded me. My present consolation is that now I no longer harbor deep remorse, and because of it, I am able to pray for forgiveness to a merciful God, Jesus Christ, whom I had rejected for years, but now I am learning to accept, love and understand.

My name is Gamaliel, a Doctor of Mosaic Law. I am over seventy years old. My eyesight is almost all gone; my health is also failing; I have all kinds of pains and aches. I have to be helped to go anywhere. I no longer talk as I used to. The last ten years of my life have been a retreat from the public life which I loved. While I suffer all the problems of old age, which I have accepted with resignation and patience, the remorse that had haunted me relentlessly, without relief, was more painful than the physical suffering and blindness

that I have now. Only by finally accepting Jesus have I been able to find the peace and joy which I needed, but did not have.

The first time I met Him, Jesus was only twelve years old. It was in the Temple in Jerusalem. For three days He questioned me, the Scribes, and the Teachers of the Law about the coming of the Messiah and what the prophets had written. We were amazed at His wisdom and knowledge. He was not an ordinary boy. He had a special innocent wisdom and humility which I had never seen in any child. He was filled with the Spirit of God. When we gave Him vague or incorrect answers, He corrected us or explained the right passages clearly and concisely. We did not expect a child to have the ability to give us clearer lessons on the Scriptures so we could have a better understanding. We were immersed in our own ignorance of what God is by not recognizing Him as an infinite and merciful God. I should have realized then and there who Jesus was! He promised me a sign then—a sign to recognize the Messiah. How blind I was! He, Himself was that sign.

I remember the death of my father, Simeon. He spent the last years of his life praying in the Temple in Jerusalem. The Spirit of God had revealed to him that he would not see death until he had set eyes on the Christ of the Lord. He proclaimed before dying that he had held in his arms, the Messiah. He did not need a sign; the Holy Spirit had guided him. He died with a smile on his face, without revealing to anyone whom he had held, or the baby's name.

I should have realized that it was Jesus that my father had held as a baby in the Temple, because he died about the same time when Jesus would have been presented in the Temple.

Eighteen years after meeting Him in the Temple, I heard again about Jesus. Amazing reports had reached me from Galilee about His teachings, the miraculous healings that He was performing, and of the expelling of demons. I decided to follow closely His whereabouts and activities. Wherever He spoke, He held the listeners spellbound. His teachings were about love, mercy, and forgiveness. No one knew where He had learned it all, or who had taught Him about the Torah and the Divine Laws. He spoke with such authority that no one could question His knowledge. To me, He still was just a simple man from Nazareth, a carpenter by trade, with no education and rejected by some of His relatives. He had selected twelve men, mostly fishermen, to be His Apostles. I did not want to recognize or accept Him as the promised Messiah.

I rejected Him completely. He was not what I had expected the Messiah to be. I had a fixed image in my selfish and vain mind of what the Messiah should be and He did not suit my criteria. I could not accept His human nature. I never recalled the words that He had said about Himself (without revealing His identity) when He was twelve years old. My pride and lack of humility continued to blind me. My ears were also closed. Although my eyes could see, the eyes of my soul and heart would not.

I should have welcomed Him when I heard He was

to come into Jerusalem and go to the Temple. Instead,
I stayed in the background and waited to see what He
would do. His first entry into His public life in the
Temple was one of anger and controversy. He forcibly
attacked the money changers, overturning their tables
and the seats of the dove sellers and then He spoke
the **TRUTH**—*"Does not the scripture say: My house
will be called a house of prayer for all peoples? But
you have turned it into a bandits' den"* (Mark 11:17).
I did not want to be involved. He had fulfilled a prophesy
and nobody could stop His wrath. The priests, Pharisees
and Scribes rushed to question Him. Now I recall His
reply—*"Destroy this Temple and I will raise it to give
glory and praise to God."* We did not understand His
answer. In a calm but forceful voice, Jesus proceeded
to warn the people about the behavior of those questioning Him. From that day on, the Pharisees, priests,
the Council, and I, myself started to attack Him, rather
than to listen to Him. Who was He to question our
authority and denounce us?

While now my physical eyes cannot see, the eyes of
my soul can. Now I can understand why I had rejected
Him. I wanted Him to be what He could never be:
a political Messiah, a militant Savior, one who would
free us, the Jewish people, from the Roman yoke and
who would make all the nations of the world subser-
vient to Judah.

Jesus' followers increased wherever He went and
whenever He spoke. He tended to the lowly, the poor,
the sick, the destitute, the hopeless, the lepers, the
prostitutes, the sinners, the needy. He filled them with

faith, hope and love. He was against the selfish, the cruel, the vain, the hypocrites, the proud, the self-righteous and those who thought that they were better than others. I was one of them. I thought that I could never be one of His disciples.

Jesus never approached the Council or the Pharisees to seek counsel. However, one of His apostles, Judas Iscariot, for whom I did not have a high respect, kept us informed of Jesus' active life. Through this miserable man the Council was able to plot and plan the moment of Jesus' capture and to submit Him to the Roman authorities for a death sentence. It took us three years to arrive at that decision.

Jesus' teaching no longer held the Talmud sacred. The Sabbath's Laws were no longer observed. Tradition was no longer followed or obeyed. In my teachings, I always said—"Provide thyself with a teacher and eschew doubtful matters, and tithe not overmuch by guesswork." I was constantly approached to explain Jesus' teachings and actions and, as a Rabban, I insisted—"Do not persist in doubt."

It was at Jesus' crucifixion and death, after three years of opposing Him, that my initial awakening occurred. Even though I had witnessed some of Jesus' miraculous physical healings; making the blind see, the lame walk, the dumb talk, the deaf hear, and finally, the resurrection of Lazarus, nothing could ever convince me. I continued to be stubborn.

It was seeing Him crucified when I felt the first remorse. I had to run like a mad man from the Temple to Golgotha, after the sign that He had promised me occurred. The Temple's veil was torn in two by a lightning bolt and a sudden earthquake cracked its walls. Fear filled me completely as I rushed in the semi-darkness of an eclipse, to ask for His forgiveness, but I arrived too late. He was already dead. My eyesight started to fade, as the semi-darkness lifted. At first, I thought it was a punishment, but it was my reluctancy to convert that kept me blind. I did not want to change and abandon my Mosaic knowledge and my reputation as a teacher. Also, I did want to protect my position at the Council and to maintain the power that I thought I had. Pure selfishness!

Time after time Jesus kept knocking at my heart's door. And time after time I would not open it. The first time I allowed Him in my heart was when I openly spoke favorably about His apostles who had been arrested. The Council wanted to sentence them to death. My eloquence convinced the Council to release them. In my weakness, I had not spoken to Peter, their leader, or to any of the apostles, nor did I allow them to talk to me about Jesus. My blindness to Jesus' prophesies blocked any desire to recognize Him. I did not want to know anything more about Jesus.

About a year after, I was furious when one of my most cherished disciples, Stephen, became a disciple of Jesus and rejected me completely. Again, I tried to make a decision about Jesus when the Council started to plot for Stephen's death. I did not want any more blood on my hands. But, Saul of Tarsus, my right hand and one of my best disciples, who had been authorized by the Council to persecute Jesus' followers, convinced the Council that Stephen be stoned to death. I did not support or participate in Stephen's death.

Shortly, after Saul departed for Damascus to arrest and persecute Jesus' followers, to my bewilderment, Saul also became a disciple of Jesus. There were many amazing stories about Saul's conversion that I did not want to believe.

I was thoroughly confused and dejected. I could no longer comprehend or be rational about Jesus. Was He truly the Messiah? If only I had opened my heart! It could have been so easy, but I did not want to admit my spiritual blindness, or clear my doubts, or correct the errors of my beliefs. The Council no longer supported me or requested my knowledge of the law on important decisions.

The world around me started to collapse. I could not be trusted, nor could I trust anyone. I retreated into my blindness and remorse took over. It lasted for years. The only alternative that I had left was to learn more about Jesus and His teachings. In seeking the answers, I had to suffer in silence. In the darkness, I accepted my physical blindness as a blessing. It opened my heart! I had to do what I had taught: Seek the teacher! Jesus! Jesus! He had all the answers!

In my prayers, I asked for faith to believe. I suddenly realized that no mortal could ever comprehend God. Who was I to question, or to deliver the many answers about the Messiah? I could not even give the right answers to a twelve-year-old!

My resentment started to melt as I started to pray

in Jesus' name. He is so merciful! He slowly allowed my soul's eyes to open; day by day He showed me where I had failed Him; the many sins I had committed and forgotten. It was as though I was reading a book of my life that revealed every single sin that I had committed. With sorrow and repentance, I kept asking for Jesus' forgiveness while my sins unfolded before my blind eyes. I would see the most beautiful light as I repented, and as I did, I would feel the most engulfing peace and joy overtake my soul. I found out later that this peace was the Holy Spirit flooding my soul with love. I did not have doubts anymore.

Love! Love! I started to learn how to return love to Jesus. His name was constantly on my lips and I no longer felt guilty or remorseful. I cannot change the past! Only love can change a person, so I must now live for the present and save my soul. Believe in Jesus Christ!

Now I understood what had happened to my two disciples Stephen and Saul. They were on fire. Now I was on fire! I no longer wanted to hide any of my feelings and thoughts about Jesus. My conversion grew stronger and I was not afraid to talk about Jesus.

Avidly I searched for knowledge from Jesus' followers and learned that Mary, Jesus' Mother, was still living in Jerusalem. I arranged to be brought to her and she did not refuse to see me. She allowed me to visit her as often as I asked. She was all that I had expected her to be. Her kindness and humility opened my heart more and more to love Jesus. She gave me, patiently, all the time that I needed and, briefly, I explained to her who I was and how I had rejected her Son. Also, I told her what had occurred to me through the years and how I finally was able to accept Jesus. She taught me like no one ever could. I no longer had any doubts. She encouraged me to be baptized so that all my sins would be forgiven. Peter, who was visiting Mary, recognized me, and baptized me without any hesitation. It was the happiest day of my life!

I decided to preach about Jesus in the Temple and to be known as a disciple of Jesus. Even though I was blind, I could be taken to the Temple and I was still respected by many people. I wanted to set Jerusalem on fire! Many of my friends warned me to stop talking about Jesus, because rumors were that many Pharisees were plotting to kill me. I was not afraid. Nothing could stop me.

EPILOGUE:

A few days after Gamaliel started to talk in the Temple, his body was found on the west side of the Temple. There were many rumors about his death. Rumors were that he had been killed, or that he committed suicide by climbing to one of the towers and threw himself down. Another, that he was taken to one of the towers, missed a step and fell to his death. He died with a small wooden cross around his neck. He was buried in the Christian graveyard.

5

Longinus

"It was Preparation Day, and to prevent the bodies remaining on the cross during the sabbath—since that sabbath was a day of special solemnity—the Jews asked Pilate to have the legs broken and the bodies taken away" (John 19:31).

It was almost three o'clock in the afternoon, when Pilate ordered a detail of soldiers to go and break the legs of the three men that had been crucified. I was in charge of the detail, since I had executed this task many times here in Judah. I am a Roman Centurian. The Jewish people had been a very rebellious race and crucifixion had been the only punishment that they could understand. The breaking of the legs causes the crucified men to die almost instantly by suffocation as they are unable to hold upward their body, but with a torturous suffering (we use a long heavy mallet and it takes only one swift swing and a blow above the ankles).

We approached the crucified men in semi-darkness because of an eclipse. One of the prisoners, whom they called Jesus, was already dead, so it was not necessary for us to inflict the painful blow. Instead, I opted to use my lance to make sure He was dead. My name is Longinus; it is Greek and it means lance.

What occurred next changed my life completely and it is impressed in my mind in vivid detail. I cannot forget it! I had been suffering of severe infections and partial loss of sight for the last year. As I pierced the right side of Jesus' chest in an upward movement to hit His heart, water and blood spurted immediately from the wound and some drops splashed my face and eyes. Instantly, I regained my sight and suddenly an earthquake occurred, as a gale from nowhere swept the area. The mob that surrounded the crucifixion site dispersed in fear. After the noise, caused by the gale, mob and earthquake subsided, an overpowering silence and calmness occurred; darkness took over. . .It was like eternity had stopped. . .Time stood still. . .Nothing moved, no noise, no singing birds, not even the wind. . . It took my breath away!

I had regained my sight, but I was frozen with fear. I wanted to run, but I could not. I could not understand what was happening, until I realized what I knew about Jesus. The Messiah. . .The Savior. . .The Son of God. . . I felt all alone with Him.

Suddenly, lightning streaked above Jerusalem, and over the crowd. As I looked up to Him a bolt hit the Temple. I saw Him all covered with blood clots, and sweat dripping from His body. His bruised flesh had

turned all blue and pale white. Nature, the earth, had sensed His death and was expressing sorrow for its Creator. Jesus!. . . Jesus!. . . Jesus!. . . Repeating His name, I knelt and proclaimed, *"Truly this man was the Son of God" (Mark* 16:39). I broke into tears; I could not stop sobbing. A deep sorrow flooded my heart, no longer had I fear, but only sadness. The darkness started to lift very slowly. I stood up and I looked up at Him again. I could only look at His face; His head was tilted to the right and His eyes were closed. I continued to sob. The terrible agony that He must have suffered was reflected in His mutilated body. Oh God!. . . Why?. . . Why?. . . Why?. . .

Joseph of Arimathea, Nicodemus the Pharisee, and Jesus' youngest apostle, John, asked me to help them to take Jesus down from the cross. I did, but handling His bloody pale dead body made me feel unworthy and contrite. After we lowered His body, Mary, Jesus' mother held His body. Oh! The sorrow of a suffering mother cannot be described. Her tears, anguish and sobbing broke my heart further. How can I forget Jesus' crucifixion after seeing Him dead, hanging from the cross, holding His body and then His Mother's suffering? I left them with reluctance, so that they could take care of Jesus' burial. Several women joined them to carry away the crucified Savior.

I had never been a religious man, but God had given me the grace to distinguish evil. I had tried to live what I thought was a righteous life. As a military man, I always conducted myself with pride and honor, never with cruelty. I was promoted through the ranks because

of my intelligence and abilities. I had met and heard
Jesus speak a few times, so I had a high respect and
reverence for Him. His teachings caused me to question all about good and evil, eternal life, Heaven and
Hell, my personal behavior. Listening to His teachings
I felt uplifted and sensed Jesus' love and kindness. I
was suprised when I received word that he had been
arrested. Him? No! It had to be a mistake. He would
be released, I thought.

The sight of His dead body, the blood and water, cause
of my regained vision, and all earthly events; an eclipse,
the severe earthquake, the gale followed by an emerg-
ing darkness, pushed me further into the overwhelming sadness within myself. The loneliness, shattered
only by the silent, distant lightning, brought forth to
me one single thought—I could not deny Him. I did
not have to have explanations, nor did I seek them;
my soul and mind knew. Yes! He is the Son of God!
"Jesus, forgive me for what I have done to You!"

It is now years after Jesus' crucifixion. I reflect with
joy and sorrow what happened to me these past years.
I am at peace within myself. Shortly after His death,
I requested to retire and to be relieved of my military
duty in the Roman Army, which was granted, and I
became a disciple of Jesus. I joined Jesus' apostles and
followed them where ever they went. Peter, the chief
of the apostles, welcomed me with open arms. I was
baptized and joined them. I gave Peter the lance that
I had used to pierce Jesus.

I was blessed to see Jesus resurrected, to witness His
ascension into Heaven and to be present at the descent

of the Holy Spirit. All of these glorious and very significant events made my faith stronger and affirmed my belief in Jesus being the Son of God. There is so much to tell about Jesus' life, but being at the foot of the cross is what I give thanks for the most to Him. At that moment of tribulation, I could have walked away and denied Him, never to think about Him again. In my sorrow, He filled me with graces. It was the gift of faith that He gave me at that moment that has made me what I am now. It changed my life.

It was not the regaining of my sight. We walk in faith. I believed for a while that God had created me only to be the one to pierce His Son's Heart; I was very remorseful. No! No!. . . I was wrong. Every time that we sin, we scourge Him, crucify Him and pierce His Heart. Jesus loves sinners. No matter how many times we sin. He will forgive us! He is Our Redeemer! Our Savior! Always forgiving! He forgave me.

We all face the choice of conversion every time we look up to Him from the foot of the cross. God continuously gives us a free will to follow His Son Jesus, or to abandon Him. Conversion is not one single act. We must constantly look to Jesus on the cross, accept our cross, prevail in our progressive conversion on the road to holiness. I had asked at the foot of the cross why He had to die? The answer is in the cross! His outstretched arms are always opened to welcome anyone who wants to follow Him—to receive from His wounded Heart drops of Blood and Water. Infinite Love and Divine Mercy!

Shortly after the descent of the Holy Spirit, Peter

explained to all the new converts, hundreds of them, that Jesus' Last Supper instituted the celebration of the Holy Eucharist on the first day of the week, on Sunday—the day He rose from the dead. No longer were we to observe the Sabbath. One more glorious day of celebration. Thank You, Jesus!

Peter explained to all the new converts what Jesus had actually said at that Passover meal and asked all of them to profess their faith in the Species, true Body and true Blood of Our Lord—the taking of Jesus' Body and Blood in the consecrated bread and wine. All the answers are in the Holy Eucharist—God's eternal covenant for all mankind. The infinite mystery of love. Jesus gives Himself totally in this sacred sacrament so that each one of us, individually, can receive His infinite love and graces for the salvation of our souls and eternal life. We must be pure and unblemished with a repentant heart to receive it. We become part of eternity as we consume His Body and Blood. He remains within us as long as our heart desires. He returns, tenfold, the love that we have for Him. We cannot ask for more, in our short life on earth, than to be part of Him.

It was in Caesarea of Cappadocia, where I was watching a sunset atop a hill overlooking the sea, when I received the gift of prayer. I was giving thanks to God for creating me and the beauty of creation, as the sun was disappearing into the horizon, changing the hue in the multiple colors of the clouds. I felt very close to Jesus, as if I had received Holy Communion. I gave thanks for the day that was fading. Then, I started to give thanks to God for all the wonderful days in my life. The love of all my family, my parents, sisters and brothers and friends. My mind wondered. I started to think of the smiles from a child, a baby. My mother holding me when I was a child; hugging her; her kind words of love. Running in the fields with my father and brothers. Scenes of love! It went on and on; it brought tears of joy in my heart. Happy moments in my life! So many! I could not give enough thanks to Jesus! I could not stop praying. It was to me the most beautiful sunset I had ever witnessed. I was in ecstasy communicating with God and He was answering me. I remained there until daybreak, when I realized what had happened to me. Peace reigned in my heart. I was to be a soldier for Jesus!

Peter celebrated the Holy Eucharist service every Sunday. I waited anxiously with an open heart for every Sunday to receive the Holy Eucharist. My life had become a life of prayer. I worked for months with the apostles, as long as I could, to help spread Jesus' teachings, but I sought only solitude and contemplation.

The joy in praying gave me the solace I needed. I asked for the Holy Spirit to guide me. I started to fast and I stopped searching. I had found my true vocation. Communion, prayer, fasting, penance and meditation. I retreated to a monastic life in Caesarea. There, guided by the Holy Spirit, I preached the word of the Lord to the people; many souls were converted. I was happy, but I encountered many hardships like "dark nights," when I felt my prayers were not being answered and seemed to be in vain. I did not feel the closeness and love from Jesus. It would last for weeks. Then it would be like rivers of rushing water. Love! Joy! Peace!

It had to be a test from God to see if I would prevail. My prayers were for the growth of the Church, the conversion of sinners, for the apostles, for the poor and so many other petitions and intentions. There was never enough time to pray. Whenever I felt empty and abandoned, I would meditate on the Passion of Our Lord. It was my cross too! I learned to trust in the Lord and His Holy Will. Some day I will see Him in all His glory. I cannot wait! I hope it is soon! He is my refuge and strength!

EPILOGUE:

There are a considerable number of stories and fables on Longinus. It is known that he suffered martyrdom and his feast is celebrated on March 15. I have only tried to write briefly about his conversion and how he might have felt, his personal emotions. It is only a short account that could be applied to any human being seeking to find himself and God. Jesus, Divine Mercy, opens our eyes first and then our heart. We have to be willing!

At least one element of the story of Longinus seems to have survived and has been recorded in a rather diabolical twist to history. That element is his spear.

The spear, after numerous transfers to specific religious centers, was housed in a museum known as the Hofburg, in Austria. It was there in the 1930s. An avowed Satanist and self-proclaimed world leader named Adolph Hitler often came to view it. It has been reported that he seemed to go into some kind of a demonic ecstasy when viewing it and revered the artifact.

In the spring of 1938, Hitler, who promoted himself to military chief in Germany, stormed through Austria and World War II was underway. He made a mad dash into Vienna and straight to the Hofburg where he confiscated his prized possession. In the spring of 1945, the Allies found and took possession of the "Spear of Longinus" in Neuremberg. It was April 30, 1945—the same day Hitler committed suicide.

6

Dismas

As I wait in the semi-darkness of this rancid, humid and solitary Roman cell, I can only think about my mother. I have been sentenced to be crucified. Whenever I had been in pain, I always thought about my mother. She was a very pious and religious woman. She always has been in my heart. She taught me how to pray. I did love her very much! Mother!... Mother!... Why do we have to suffer so in this life?

Before she died, her last request was for me to memorize a beautiful psalm that she always prayed, and to recite it whenever I faced any danger. She said it would give me strength and hope. I remember her words: **"Dismas**, be a good boy! Think of me when you recite it."

"I let you down mother, please forgive me! I am ashamed of what I have been. A thief, a robber and, now, a convict to be crucified.

I memorized the psalm before she died to make her
happy and give her peace in her heart. I pray part of
it now:

> *"I love the LORD because He has heard
> my voice in supplication, because He has in-
> clined His ear to me the day I called. The
> cords of death encompassed me; the snares
> of the nether world seized upon me; I fell into
> distress and sorrow, and I called upon the
> name of the Lord, 'O Lord, save my life!'. . .
> Gracious is the Lord and just; yes, our God
> is merciful. The Lord keeps the little ones;
> I was brought low, and He saved me. Return,
> O my soul, to your tranquility, for the Lord
> has been good to you. For He has freed my
> soul from death, my eyes from tears, my feet
> from stumbling. I shall walk before the Lord
> in the land of the living."*

My mother died shortly after my father did. Her death
was caused more by the sorrow of his death than from
the illness that she had. She loved my father very much.
Looking back at my life, there was so much despair,
pain, sorrow, and suffering. What is life and death? I
never understood why both of my parents had to suffer
and die so young. They were God fearing people. As
for myself, I *do* understand why I have to die—I am
a criminal. I have to pay for my crimes.

My parents and I lived on a small farm in the south-
ern part of Judea. My father was a good man, kind to
my mother and I. He was loved by everyone, until my

mother contacted "the fever." Doctors could not do anything for her. As soon as word got around of her illness, we were treated like lepers. Nobody dared to come
near us or to the house. None of our relatives or friends
would help us. Everybody was afraid of "the fever." My
father no longer could manage the farm, he could only
take care of my mother. I helped as much as I could,
but then father also became ill, so I had to take care
of both. Father had some savings, but soon he ran out
of money paying the doctors. I did not know what to
do! I had to feed my parents. Without them knowing,
I would sneak out at night to steal food from the town's
market or from the neighbors. Things could not be
worse. Mother never gave up hope, and she kept her
faith until the last minute of her life. God was kind
to me, but I did not know that then. Both of my parents died within days of each other. I buried both on
my father's farm. No more suffering for them! My only
consolation was that I was able to take care of them.
I cried for days!

My sorrow and despair, after the death of my parents, turned into anger, hatred and resentment. In time
of need nobody gave us help. Where was God when
I needed Him the most? I abandoned God. I had lost
my faith in people and in God. I stopped praying, even
the psalm that I had memorized, for I did not really
understand its meaning. I had to get away as far as
I could from the area where I had lived.

Judea had been under Roman occupation for years
and had been governed by Herod, a half Jew and a
despot. Rebels were constantly fighting the Romans.

The whole country was in a turmoil. My first thought was to join a band of rebels, insurgents, but I was too young to fight. I did not know anyone and I did not have any money. Only the will to live! I decided to steal from the Synagogue. I was able to sneak in and steal various bags of coins left as offerings. On the outskirts of the town I managed to steal a camel. Both acts punishable by death. I did not care! I headed for Jerusalem. Supposedly it had many beautiful sights, especially the Temple.

It took me two days to get to Jerusalem. I became afraid as I approached the outskirts. The road was filled with crosses of crucified rebels and criminals. A chill ran down my spine as I approached one that was delirious. He must have been on the cross for days. He kept muttering: "Let me die! Let me die!"

The irony of it all! I know now why such a great fear swept through me upon seeing that crucified man. I would be suffering the same punishment.

I did not enter Jerusalem, but continued traveling north and joined a pilgrim's caravan. The caravan master somehow took sympathy on me, because of my age, and asked me to work for him. It was the first kind act that I had received from a stranger.

It was a new experience for me to work. I tried to do everything to please him and I worked hard. My job was to take care of the camels, donkeys and horses. The caravan master was an astute merchant trading throughout Judea. He was an infidel, but managed to organize pilgrimages to Jerusalem. He had interest in the Jewish religion and would come to me to learn the little that I knew. I told him all that my mother had taught me. His questions made me realize how little I knew about God and my religion. He had many questions about the Messiah which I could not answer.

At the Temple, I was amazed at the vast number of people gathered to celebrate religious feasts, especially Passover. I would ask myself many questions. There had to be a God!

I worked for a few years for the caravan master and I learned that he was not an honest man. He overcharged the poor people and stole from them. From the wages he was to pay me, in turn he would charge me for the food, which left me with nothing. I began to hate him.

We had to be on constant guard from bands of robbers. On more than one occasion we were attacked and robbed, until a fatal day the entire caravan was massacred. I was wounded and the robbers, instead of killing me, offered me my life if I joined them. What could I do, but to resign to a new kind of life? I did not want to die!

I had a hard time getting used to being a robber. No honor or trust. I learned to fight for my life and to be brutal. Reflecting on it, I am ashamed. Slowly I became a criminal without a heart.

Looking back at those many years, I can only recall one incident when I was merciful. It was many years ago, about thirty years. We were headed toward Bethlehem, when we caught sight of a lonely traveling couple with an infant child. They were headed toward Egypt. I cannot forget the courage of the man. He was

ready to defend his wife and child with his life. Seeing
them defenseless, I stopped the attack by persuading
the leader of the band to leave them alone. In return,
I would give up all my share of the last raid for their
lives. I will never forget the **woman.** She had a beauty
and serenity that I never had seen before. I managed
to talk to them for few moments and gave them direc-
tions for a safer and shorter route to Egypt. The man
sensed what I had done and gave me thanks with a
hug. His boy child in turn hugged one of my legs. I
remember the last words the man said as they departed.

"God, in His mercy, will reward you for what you
have done tonight."

The next day we learned that Herod had ordered to
kill all boys under two years of age.

We disbanded into small groups whenever the
Romans were on our tracks. But somehow the Romans
learned about our meeting place and were waiting for
us. We had been betrayed by an informer.

The whole gang was condemned to forced labor,
building roads and aqueducts. It was years of physical
suffering. I was mistreated, beaten, scourged, starved
and treated worse than any slave. Man can be the crue-
lest of all animals! I accepted my fate without com-
plaints. The psalms helped me.

During a sudden unexpected sand storm, I managed
to escape. Being free, I decided to change, although,
I was bitter at life. All I had known was dishonesty,
cruelty, lying, and cheating. There had to be something
good in life! I did not want any more crimes on my
conscience. I kept remembering my mother's words!

I had hidden some of the loot from the robberies
and with it, I was able to take on a new identity and
bought a small farm in Galilee. My life took a different course. I became an honest man. I was happy for
the first time in my life.

Then something wonderful happened, for which I
give thanks to God with my whole heart. It was about
a year ago, when I heard **Jesus** speak. I had heard of
Him before and was curious as to what kind of man
He was. His name was mentioned wherever I went.
Ever since that day, I realized how worthless my life
had been. My conscience was awakened. I felt guilty
and remorseful of what I had done and I wanted to
atone. His words filled me with joy and peace. He
promised eternal life. Life after death!

Now, in this cell, I think about what He said, and
begin to understand what life and death are. Life
includes suffering, but is only a flash of eternity. Insig-
nificant! How can I deserve eternity? By doing God's
will. Sin is not doing His will. I must repent for my
sins. When I did His will, I was filled with love. Love
opens all doors. Oh Jesus! Thank You Jesus! Now I
understand the psalm words.

I wanted to follow Jesus, but I could not do it. How
could I? I was an escaped convict. If recognized it would
be the end of me. I wanted to learn as much as possible about Him. To many, He was a new prophet, to
others the promised Messiah. To me, He was the hope
my mother spoke of.

I remember something extraordinary that happened
once. How could I forget it? After Jesus finished preach-

ing, He always laid hands on the sick people. Near me was a blind old woman, a beggar in dirty old clothes. She wanted to be near Jesus. None would touch or help her. I decided to help her, and guided her close to Jesus. Oh Jesus! I cannot forget the look in Your eyes as You looked at me and what You said to me:

"God in his Mercy will reward you for what you have done tonight."

He then proceeded to spit on the tip of His fingers and touched the old woman's eyes. She was immediately cured. I started to cry with joy.

I realized the next day, that the words He said to me were the same words I had heard thirty years before. I was stunned.

A few months later, a neighbor rushed to tell me that Jesus was in the city. I went with him immediately and as we arrived at the gate of the town, we were challenged by the Roman guards on duty. My heart sank. I recognized one of the guards as one of the camp guards, where I had escaped from. He recognized me, also, and arrested me. In chains, I was sent to Jerusalem for trial. It was a quick trial. The guard testified who I was and I was sentenced to be crucified on the day before the Feast of Passover.

That is the story of my past. Now, I let you live, with me, the present.

It is late at night and I am taken out of the cell and placed in chains in another cell with two other convicts. We are to be crucified tomorrow. One of the convicts is Barabbas, a well-known criminal, and a murderer. The other convict is a member of his band.

All they do is curse God. I avoid talking to them. Since I only have but a few hours, I pray for forgiveness. I am no longer afraid of death.

The next day, early in the morning, Barabbas is taken out of the cell. The Roman guards return empty-handed to tell us that Barabbas has been pardoned by the Roman Procurator, Pontius Pilate. The Romans usually release a prisoner to please the crowd, as they celebrate the Feast of Passover. The other convict and I are taken out into a large yard. I am blinded by the sunlight. There is a third man to be crucified with us. I am to be at the rear of the procession. I take my cross, which is very heavy, and we proceed to enter the street. There is a mob like I have never seen before. Yelling and cursing! They all behave worse than animals and the soldiers have to use horses to disperse the crowd. I try to block out the noise of the crowd. Their ire is for the convict leading the procession. I hear His name. It is Jesus!. . . Oh!. . . No!. . . No!. . . I cannot recognize Him! What have they done to Him? He has been scourged and is wearing a crown of thorns. Why?. . . Why Him?. . .

Three times we stop to rest, because Jesus falls to the ground exhausted. I can hardly distinguish the people ahead of me, drops of sweat get into my eyes. I am used to corporal pain, but Jesus must be suffering excruciating pain from the wood of the cross rubbing against the scourged wounds, the weight of the cross, and the crown in His head. Please God assist Him!

We finally arrive at the place where we are going to be crucified, a mount on the outskirts of Jerusalem.

I am the first to be crucified, followed by Barabbas'
associate. I am in too much pain to be aware of the
events around me. All I hear is blasphemies, insults
and cursing addressed to Jesus. Oh Jesus! You gave them
love and this is what they do to You. Why?... Why?...

Jesus is crucified and the Roman soldiers raise up
His cross in the center of the mount. I am on His left
side and I can hear Him say:

*"Father, forgive them; they do not know what they
are doing."*

Barabbas' associate blasphemes Him:

"Aren't you the Messiah? Then save Yourself and us."

I rebuked him:

"Have you no fear of God, seeing you are under the
same sentence? We deserve it, after all. We are paying
the price for what we've done, but this man has done
nothing wrong."

I look at Jesus and say:

"Jesus, remember me when You enter upon Your
reign."

Jesus replies:

*"I assure you, this day you will be with me in para-
dise."* (*Luke* 23:34, 39-43).

I faint upon hearing Jesus' words, but before fainting
I feel an undescribable joy and peace. "Jesus! Jesus! I
love You! I lay my life into Your hands!"

When I wake up, it is all over. Jesus is dead, and
I am surrounded by darkness, and shortly after:

"Mother, father, I shall walk before the LORD in the
land of the living."

The Stations of the Cross

by Laurie Balbach-Taylor

Faith Publishing Company

Most generous Heavenly Father, as we meditate with our hearts on the passion of Your only Son, may we turn in loving gratitude to You. May our Heavenly Mother help us to understand the suffering and death on the Cross Your Son obediently endured out of love for us. Send us Your Holy Spirit that He may bestow on us the grace to honor Jesus' passion with the fervor we should have as undeserving heirs to eternal life.

We surrender ourselves to You with the aid of Holy Mary, through our Lord, Jesus Christ, Who lives and reigns with You and the Holy Spirit, one God for ever and ever. Amen.

The First Station: *Jesus is condemned to death.*

Our dear Lord's trial was unfair. He was betrayed and abandoned by His friends.

As God, He knew that He was embarking on the most significant event in human history. He needed to proceed in order that we might be reconciled with the Father. As man, though, He felt the sting of desolation, being left utterly devoid of friendly compassion as He faced a cowardly politician who catered to the whims of a mob.

Justice was not to be found here. Jesus was wrongly declared a criminal and sentenced to death. Our sins and transgressions against the laws of God are so horrid that they cried out for the purest, most innocent, perfect atonement. In the eyes of the Father, no one less than Jesus would suffice.

We adore You, O Christ, and we praise You, because by Your holy Cross, You have redeemed the world.

The Second Station: *Jesus carries His Cross.*

His love so great that He could not refuse the Father—or us—Jesus hoisted the wood of His Cross onto His pure yet badly scourged shoulder, carrying the burden of the whole world's sins. Love this great had never been seen before, and it would never be seen again.

The pain was intense as the wooden beam dug deep into the raw, open flesh of our Lord's precious body. The salty sweat of intense suffering poured into all His wounds, burning Jesus' sacred torso, while the weight of the Cross gouged to the bone.

The pain was excruciating, yet Jesus continued to love. His love kept Him moving forward, through the narrow streets of Jerusalem to the hill of Golgotha—to Calvary, where He would be executed.

We adore You, O Christ, and we praise You, because by Your holy Cross, You have redeemed the world.

The Third Station: *Jesus falls the first time.*

How much can one man bear? Jesus suffered from lack of sleep, a brutal beating which ravaged His flesh, and even a crown of thorns jammed onto His head. The crowd jeered at Him.

As He carried the weight of all the sins of the world on His precious shoulders, He stumbled, and the crowd laughed as He collapsed in the dust of the road. They mocked Him and spit on Him as He pulled Himself up. He knew that His task was more important than answering the crowd's abuse.

He loved even those who ridiculed Him. He embraced the Cross for love of them and for all people like them, who, throughout all the ages, would make fun of His agonizing love for us. His obedience to the Father would repay our ungrateful disobedience. His love would overwhelm our indifference.

We adore You, O Christ, and we praise You, because by Your holy Cross, You have redeemed the world.

The Fourth Station: *Jesus meets His mother.*

No loving son can bear the lines of grief etched into the face of His mom. Jesus' torture was augmented further when He saw the heartache His Mother was enduring. But Mary was carrying her grief along with His as her presence supported His decision to continue along the path to His death. Her grief over His suffering and her own knowledge of His doom wracked her sorrowful heart, and the anguish showed in her eyes.

As Mother embraced her Son, the dust, sweat, and blood covering Him mingled with the tears that she shed. The pain of the Cross was being shared by this

most holy woman, who had helped Him grow to this
point in life. He praised the Father for the comfort of
Mary's presence as He continued His journey, even as
her consolation increased His pain because of His compassion for her.

His love for her—and for us—gave Him the strength
to move on.

*We adore You, O Christ, and we praise You, because
by Your holy Cross, You have redeemed the world.*

The Fifth Station: *Simon of Cyrene helps Jesus carry
the Cross.*

Along the way, our precious Savior knew His human
strength was failing. In His weakness, pain, and fatigue,
He allowed Simon of Cyrene to help Him carry His
Cross.

As Simon lifted the Cross, he was distraught at its
weight. As he began walking, it amazed him that a man
as brutally disfigured as Jesus could have carried it so far
already. No mere mortal can know fully, at least in his
lifetime, what importance such assistance would be.

Simon could not have known that he carried the
Cross on which his sins and all the sins which ever
were or ever would be committed would be atoned.
He was unaware of the grace he had received in being
forced into service in such a way. Jesus' love for him
sustained Simon, as it sustains us even today.

*We adore You, O Christ, and we praise You, because
by Your holy Cross, You have redeemed the world.*

The Sixth Station: *Veronica wipes the face of Jesus.*

Veronica's heart melted in grief for this innocent Man being led like a lamb to the slaughter. She saw the dusty blood and sweat running into His eyes. His tears could not wash the grit away, and He could hardly see the path before Him.

In her compassion, Veronica took a cloth and cleaned the mess from the holy face of our Lord. She risked the ridicule of the mob for daring to show concern for a condemned criminal. Her love for Jesus was imprinted in that moment on His heart.

In gratitude for her service, the Lord imprinted His image on the cloth—yet another testimony of His great love for us.

We adore You, O Christ, and we praise You, because by Your holy Cross, You have redeemed the world.

The Seventh Station: *Jesus falls the second time.*

As He staggered once again, Jesus fell onto the filty roadway. The brutal soldiers whipped Him, as if that would give Him the strength to get up and move on.

Jesus struggled again to His feet. His love for even these captors was too great to allow Him to tarry when the Father's will awaited fulfillment.

In His merciful heart, He begged the Father for forgiveness for His persecutors—and for us all—as He experienced an overwhelming love for all mankind, even those who tortured Him so cruelly. His love for all His tormentors continues throughout eternity.

We adore You, O Christ, and we praise You, because by Your holy Cross, You have redeemed the world.

The Eighth Station: *Jesus consoles the women of Jerusalem.*

As Jesus approached the women of Jerusalem who waited for Him along the path to Calvary, He momentarily forgot His own pain and suffering as He saw the grief written on their faces. These women were His friends. They had supported Him in His preaching. Now they offered their support in His most important task of His ministry.

In his compassion for the women, He paused along the path to speak with them, offering them words of consolation. He was overwhelmed with love for them— and for us—as He comforted them in their anxiety, and continued on His road to death.

We adore You, O Christ, and we praise You, because by Your holy Cross, You have redeemed the world.

The Ninth Station: *Jesus falls the third time.*

His journey to Calvary almost complete, Jesus stumbled on the slopes of that fateful hill and fell yet again. The weight of the Cross had taken its toll on His human body.

As the soldiers prodded Him, Jesus looked around disconsolately. He saw His Mother, Mary, and His apostle, John. He saw such a meager handful of friends who had dared to risk going this far with Him. In His fatigue and pain, He saw with bleary eyes the heartache His few remaining relatives and friends were experiencing out of their love for Him.

He knew it was not over yet. The last few steps up the hill were before Him. He again picked up the Cross, staggered to His feet, and resolutely continued the climb out of love for these few—and for all people, including us.

We adore You, O Christ, and we praise You, because by Your holy Cross, You have redeemed the world.

The Tenth Station: *Jesus is stripped of His garments.*

The Cross bearing our sins, awaiting its precious cargo, lay on the hill. Our innocent Savior stood nearby, as the soldiers converged to prepare Him for death.

They stripped Him of His clothing, being careful not to rip their own spoils, but caring nothing about the pain they caused their Victim. Jesus' battered flesh bled afresh as the soldiers roughly pulled the tunic from His skin. His back and shoulders shuddered in pain. His knees, which had so often knelt in prayer to the Father, were bloodied from His falls.

As the dark clouds gathered in the sky, God the Father beheld His innocent Son, in absolute obedience, deprived of every shred of dignity, awaiting His immolation. The Father saw that the Sacrifice was good—was the best—was utterly perfect. The love of the Father for the Son radiated from the eyes of Jesus, and was felt in the heart of our humble Savior, as He gazed through history in love at all humanity.

We adore You, O Christ, and we praise You, because by Your holy Cross, You have redeemed the world.

The Eleventh Station: *Jesus is nailed to the Cross.*

The soldiers hurled their loving Victim onto the wood on the ground. They had been drinking and were unnecessarily rough. They needed to bolster their courage to perform this indecent final torture on this good

and holy Man. They needed to justify themselves in
the eyes of the pitiful onlookers.

They held our dear Jesus down, grating His open flesh
against the rough wood of the Cross. As He writhed
in pain, the soldiers pounded the rough nails into His
precious hands and feet, adhering the Savior to the sins
of the world. He willingly became One with our transgressions in order to free us from our guilt.

And His love for His tormentors flowed in waves of
pain as He sacrificed Himself out of His love for all
mankind. His perfect, pure, and holy love, displayed
in His humility and obedience to the Father, reconciled our prideful disobedience.

*We adore You, O Christ, and we praise You, because
by Your holy Cross, You have redeemed the world.*

The Twelfth Station: *Jesus dies on the Cross.*

As Jesus, on His Cross, was lifted into place for all
passerbys to see, His Mother, Mary, offered her pure
white veil to shield any degree of modesty which could
be preserved in His pitiable state. His heart was breaking with the love He felt for her—and for us all—as
He gently accepted her ministrations to Him and offered
those ministrations to all of us. In His agony, He
remembered the people for whom He was sent to die,
and He gave His Mother to us as our own spiritual
Mother. He remembered, too, to provide for her needs
in His absence by delivering her into the care of His
loyal apostle, John.

He shouted to the Father to forgive His torturers in
their ignorance. He prayed to the Father to forgive us
all for the indifference mankind would always display

for His supreme act of sacrifice.

Bearing the iniquities of us all, He abandoned Himself into the care of the Father and released His Spirit in the greatest outpouring of love the world would ever know. *We adore You, O Christ, and we praise You, because by Your holy Cross, You have redeemed the world.*

The Thirteenth Station: *Jesus is taken down from the Cross.*

After He was already dead, the soldier pierced the side of the innocent Victim, and blood and water gushed forth, permeating the ground beneath His body. It was a cleansing of the world which, even as He was dying, He had known most of humanity throughout the ages would not appreciate.

The soldiers removed the Body so that It would not remain hanging on the Sabbath. It was placed in the arms of the Victim's grieving Mother, who lovingly caressed the tattered and torn skin as she gazed in utter dejection on the pale, lifeless face of her Offspring. Tears wrenched the Mother's heart and dripped onto the lifeless form in her lap. She rocked the Body back and forth, remembering the many times before when she had cradled the little Boy who had lovingly played and learned there in her motherly shelter. She accepted her grief and offered it to God, uniting it to the finished suffering of this noble, most worthy, and totally undeserving Victim.

She knew, too, that her work of teaching and loving would continue for all mankind, as was her Son's dying wish.

We adore You, O Christ, and we praise You, because by Your holy Cross, You have redeemed the world.

The Fourteenth Station: *Jesus is laid in the sepulcher.*

The Lamb of God had been slain. He was sacrificed for the sins of the world in a new and perfect Passover.

The loving relatives and friends of Jesus and Mary regained enough courage to approach the holy, anguished Mother, weeping over the precious cargo in her lap. As she cried such bitter tears over her loss, they gently lifted the Body away from her and began preparing It for entombment.

After wrapping the lifeless Body of our dear Savior in clean burial linens, they laid It so reverently in a new tomb. They rolled the boulder against the opening, sealing the Body in Its final earthly resting place, and the dejected followers of Jesus went their ways home in the gathering twilight. Their hope in Him was dashed. They would not understand the power of His love for them—and for us—for three days...

Our Father...; Hail Mary...; Glory be...;